RILEY CAN'T STOP CRYING

RILEY CAN'T STOP CRYING

Stéphanie Boulay

illustrated by
Agathe Bray-Bourret

translated by
Charles Simard

ORCA BOOK PUBLISHERS

Thanks

For the first look and the first drive,
thank you to Jennifer Tremblay. And for the first readings,
thank you to Nadine Boulay, Mathis Bouffard and Samuele.
— S.B.

Text copyright © Stéphanie Boulay 2018, 2021
Illustrations copyright © Agathe Bray-Bourret 2018, 2021
Translation copyright © Charles Simard 2021

Published in Canada and the United States in 2021 by Orca Book Publishers.
Originally published in French in 2018 by Les éditions Fonfon under the title *Anatole qui ne séchait jamais*. All rights reserved.
orcabook.com

Library and Archives Canada Cataloguing in Publicationa
Title: Riley can't stop crying / Stéphanie Boulay ;
illustrated by Agathe Bray-Bourret ; translated by Charles Simard.
Other titles: Anatole qui ne séchait jamais. English | Riley cannot stop crying
Names: Boulay, Stéphanie, 1987- author. | Bray-Bourret, Agathe, illustrator. |
Simard, Charles, 1983- translator.
Description: Translation of: Anatole qui ne séchait jamais.
Identifiers: Canadiana (print) 20200274635 | Canadiana (ebook) 20200274643 |
ISBN 9781459826380 (hardcover) | ISBN 9781459826397 (PDF) | ISBN 9781459826403 (EPUB)
Classification: LCC PS8603.O9359 A8313 2021 | DDC jc843/.6—dc23

Library of Congress Control Number: 2020939268

Summary: While his sister tries everything to help, a young boy isn't
sure why he can't stop crying in this transitional picture book.

Orca Book Publishers is committed to reducing the consumption
of nonrenewable resources in the making of our books. We make
every effort to use materials that support a sustainable future.

Orca Book Publishers gratefully acknowledges the support for its publishing
programs provided by the following agencies: the Government of Canada,
the Canada Council for the Arts and the Province of British Columbia
through the BC Arts Council and the Book Publishing Tax Credit.

We acknowledge the financial support of the Government of Canada through
the National Translation Program for Book Publishing, an initiative of the
*Roadmap for Canada Official Languages 2013-2018: Education, Immigration,
Communities,* for our translation activities.

Artwork created using watercolor and gouache

Edited by Liz Kemp
Translated by Charles Simard
Design by Ella Collier
Cover and interior artwork by Agathe Bray-Bourret

Printed and bound in China.

24 23 22 21 • 1 2 3 4

TO YOU WHO FEEL DIFFERENT
YOU ARE PERFECT
AS YOU ARE.
—S.B.

My little brother
had just turned four,
and he was crying a lot.
That's all he ever did. In the
morning he cried. In the afternoon
he cried. While he was eating or
sleeping, while it was sunny outside and
while everyone else was looking happy and
saying hello to one another, he was crying.

Dad and I would say his name
and make all sorts of funny faces.

"Riley, Riley."

He cried.

We would smear a thousand colors on our faces and make all sorts of animal sounds.

He cried.

We would sing funny songs and shake
our bodies all over the place.

"There once was a chap who could only yap,

HEE-HAAAW! HEE-HAAAAW!"

He just kept crying.

We'd ask him,

"Riley, why are you crying?"

He'd answer,
"Don't know."
It was always the same answer.
"Don't know."

Dad got discouraged and didn't know what to do. He would hold his head in his hands for hours, not saying a word. He stopped paying attention to me, and I thought he might soon start crying as loudly as Riley.

I am Regina Bibeau, Riley's older sister, and I can take care of lots of things all by myself. I can brush my teeth, brush my hair, make fishtail braids and draw trees that look like giant cauliflowers. I can read books with lots of words, draw sea lions, study mosquitoes with a magnifying glass, choose appropriate layers of clothing and take good care of my pets. But I was starting to wish I had a dad who didn't hold his head, and a little brother whose eyes were dry so that we could go for walks to the corner store and drink juice through a straw and be happy.

It seemed like Riley wasn't ever, ever going
to stop crying, so I needed to find out what
was wrong. I thought about it for a long, long
time—and then I got an idea.

I found all sorts of pencils, pens, crayons and felt-tip markers, and also paintbrushes and a watercolor kit.

I put it all on the kitchen table and started drawing. And painting. I drew and painted all day long.

One picture for everything that
might make a little kid cry. All the
sad and scary things I could think of,
I showed them in my art.

A head that hurt.

Arms, legs and
feet that hurt.

A belly that hurt.

Teeth that hurt.

A blue-and-yellow monster

under Dad's bed.

Our babysitter, Lola
(who looks like an alien).

A big
mean dog.

The night.

A ghost.

A closet.

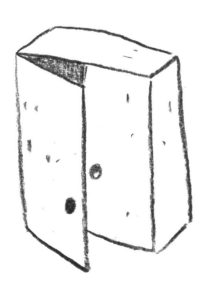

Mom (we don't know much about her, so I made up some parts).

I showed my pictures to Riley and asked him to point to what made him cry. But none of them did, and Riley cried even harder. When he calmed down, he asked me for a sheet of paper and some crayons. That's when something extraordinary happened.

He drew a little boy who looked just
like him and then said, "Riley."

"Oh! Riley, is it your name
that makes you cry?"

"No, it's Riley."

"Okay..."

At first I didn't understand. But then I had
another idea, and I told Dad about it.

"Daddy, I think Riley is crying
because he's not happy being Riley."

Dad didn't really believe me. He said such feelings were too complicated for my little brother. But I was sure, even if Dad wasn't.

I get that I'm just a kid, but with everything I *did* know, even if it isn't a whole lot, I thought I understood something about the things that are really important in life.

Once, at school, Sarah Lalonde told me I had a big belly and should stop eating french fries. Her mother had taught her that fries make you fat and that being fat is bad. So when I got home, I looked at myself in the mirror to see if what Sarah had said was true. It was—I did have a big, round belly.

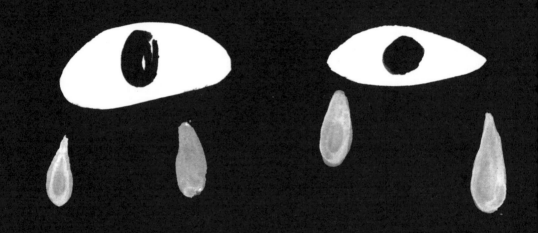

For the first time in my life, I wasn't happy being Regina Bibeau. That made me cry hard, alone in the dark. I cried so hard that Dad heard me and came to ask what was wrong.

And that's when my dad taught me something
I'll never forget.

"Regina, you like to run, swim, dance, sing and
draw, right?"

"Right."

"And you know that your body can do all
those things because it's strong and healthy,
right?"

"Right."

"And you like to drink water and eat
vegetables, beans, rice and sometimes french
fries and chocolate, right?"

"Right."

"Does it feel like your body is happy with the
food you give it? Does it show you it's happy
by making you grow and laugh and jump?"

"Yes!"

"If you pay attention to what your body tells you, and if you feel happy and healthy, you'll be as strong and amazing as children are meant to be. It's not what your body looks like that's important, it's how you take care of it. And it takes care of you by letting you do what you love to do in life. Your body is the garden in which you grow all the wonderful things about yourself that make you *you*!"

I totally understood what Dad meant. And if it was true for me, maybe it was true for my brother too. Did Riley have a body that felt comfortable to him? When I looked at him, I thought he did. Was he healthy? Could he play, go for walks, draw? Yes. So what was it that made Riley not want to be *Riley*?

One day when Riley was crying as usual,
I asked him if he liked his own thoughts.

If he tried to think about only nice things like insects, tulips and popcorn, would it make him cry less, even for five minutes?

Riley didn't know.

I placed my hand over his eyes so he could
empty his mind, and I tried to make him think
of beautiful things.

I talked about grassy hills, beach balls,
a beautiful light-brown horse and
maple-sugar candy.

Riley still cried.

Another day I asked Riley if he liked his
clothes. He didn't know. So we looked
at some clothing stores together. Riley
decided he really liked overalls, cowboy
boots, skirts and baseball shirts. I talked
to Dad, and we decided to order Riley
some clothes he liked.

(At first, Dad didn't want to buy him
the yellow skirt. He said skirts were
for little girls like me, not for little
boys. But I pointed out that I often
wore pants and shirts just like his
and Riley's. Dad said I was right
and this was true.)

Click! We ordered the skirt
and everything else Riley liked.

Riley didn't cry for the rest of the day.

The next day I asked Riley, who was
crying again, if he liked his heart. Since
he didn't know, we listened to it using my
stethoscope. His heart seemed to be in the
right place and had a good beat—the same
as mine anyway. Which was a good thing. I
wouldn't have wanted his heart to be broken,
and I didn't think I could have cured him, even
with all the tools in my doctor's kit.

Then another time I asked him if he liked his toys. We put all our toys in a big pile on the floor and looked at them.

I told him to pick out the ones he
liked and leave those he didn't.

He picked out a lot—his fire truck, our coloring books, my rainbow pony, my slushie-making machine, his toolbox, my magic wand and our jelly spiders.

He didn't want his kite, his construction helmet, his LEGO bricks or his miniature jungle animals anymore. Which was good news for me—I liked all those toys. We played with our traded toys until dinnertime, and Riley was really happy about his new treasures.

Another day we shaved Riley's head on the sides, and I got to dye two locks of my hair pink, one on each side. My teacher, Mrs. Marcelle, wanted me to change mine back to how it was, like the other kids' hair. Dad spent at least forty-five minutes in the principal's office arguing that I should have the right to do what I wanted with my hair. I could hear them from the hallway.

Mrs. Marcelle screamed that I wouldn't be a good role model for others if I was too different. (Some people really have weird ideas.) But our babysitter, Lola, *loved* our new hairstyles and gave us lots of compliments.

We painted Riley's room in sunshine yellow and mine in apple green, which was better than the azure blue and cotton-candy pink they were before.

Riley began wearing his new clothes—the overalls, the skirt, the baseball shirt. He rotated through his favorite outfits every week.

For accessories, I gave him some
multicolored plastic bracelets and my
superhero sunglasses. He looked very
colorful and very beautiful. But he
didn't look like the other boys.

I noticed when we were out that people looked at us much more than they had before, in the street, at the grocery store, at the park, in the movie theater.

Some people winked and others giggled.
Some looked at us the way Sarah Lalonde
looked at me and whispered to their
friends.

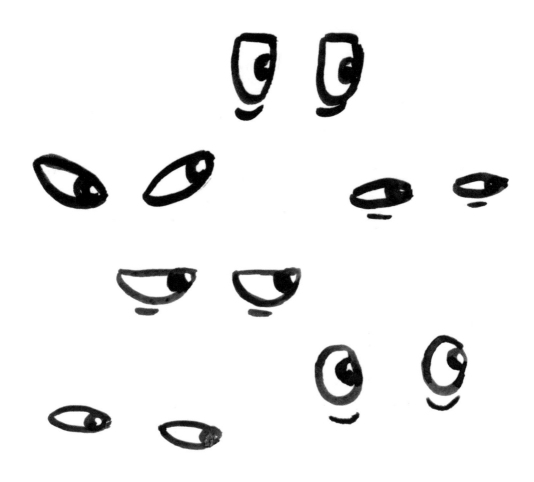

Riley was too young to notice it, but I wasn't, and Dad wasn't either. Dad decided the best way to deal with these people was to be extra nice. "Hello! Hello!" he'd call out as we walked by.

HELLO!!

HELLO!!

61

Our days were changing, and the three
of us laughed a lot. The whole family had
changed—me with my pink streaks, Riley
with his rock-and-roll haircut, and Dad with
no need to hold his head in his hands.

63

Of course, my little brother still cries
sometimes. In the morning or in the evening
or both. I think this is because we can
express some of ourselves on the outside,
but there will always be complicated things
inside ourselves that we don't know how to
show. So Riley and I, we've been creating
little ways to take care of our hearts. And
our gardens, where all sorts of flowers grow
together, like geraniums and daisies and
dandelions (which are three beautiful kinds
of flowers that are very different from each
other and definitely aren't roses).

Life doesn't always work out perfectly like in fairy tales, but I don't like those stories that much anyway.

Every time someone makes a mean face at Riley, or Sarah Lalonde makes me feel bad, or Dad has to argue with another adult about who we are, every time I miss Mom, every time Mrs. Marcelle tells me to get my head out of the clouds, I think that maybe as people get older, they stop trying to grow their gardens. They stop celebrating all the special things that make them **them**.

♪ ♪ ♪
♪ ♪ ♪
"There once was a chap who could only yap,

And so I say hello to everyone I can.
And I sing a lot—and loudly! And I tickle
Riley under his armpits. And I look at my
family and think to myself that together,
the three of us, hand in hand—we make
the greatest band! (I like this ending
because it rhymes!)

HEE-HAAAW! HEE-HAAAAW!"

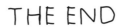

Author and singer-songwriter **Stéphanie Boulay** is half of the Québécois folk group Les soeurs Boulay. When she's not writing music, she's writing award-winning books for readers of all ages that encourage them to be whatever makes them most happy. Stéphanie lives in Montreal.

Born and raised in Montreal, **Agathe Bray-Bourret** studied cinema at Concordia University before her passion for drawing made her change floors and enrol in film animation instead, the perfect mix of her two passions. She uses watercolor and gouache to show the humor of everyday life. Currently Agathe is illustrating a graphic novel and an animated short movie. She lives in Montreal.

Prospect Heights Public Library
12 N. Elm Street
Prospect Heights, IL 60070
www.phpl.info